I0554204

# What Lies Beneath

## A Series of Stories by

### Coco

## Illustration by

### Mario Bloom

DJD Publications

Jacksonville, Florida

**What Lies Beneath**
**DJD Publications**
**Jacksonville, Florida**
cococamwrites@aol.com

DJD Publications Books are available at special discounts for bulk purchases. Contact: Coco at www.cocorobertsbooks.com

# Table Of Contents

Table Of Contents ........................................................4

    Ethan and Stacie ..............................................1

Chapter 1 ....................................................................1

Chapter 2 ....................................................................6

Chapter 3 ....................................................................9

Chapter 4 ..................................................................25

Chapter 5 ..................................................................41

Chapter 6 ..................................................................58

    The Walberg's .................................................68

Chapter 1 ..................................................................68

Chapter 2 ..................................................................73

Chapter 3 ..................................................................81

    The Rather's ...................................................90

Chapter 1 ..................................................................90

Chapter 2 ................................................................100

Chapter 3 ................................................................106

Chapter 4 ................................................................111

*Ethan and Stacie*

# **<u>Chapter 1</u>**

Ethan was handsome, sexy and charming, with a smile that could melt the coldest heart and the body of a Greek God! When he opened his mouth to speak, there's an instant waterfall in my panties! This man was fine, with a capital F. The good Lord seemed to have made this man with the most sacred, the most beautiful, strongest mortar that he owned.

I met Ethan a few months back, while I was trying to stick to my New Year's resolution in the gym. I could barely concentrate on doing my usual workout whenever I saw him. He caught me starring once and flashed me an award-winning smile. "Damn!" I started talking to myself. "Stacie, girl, you have got to get it together." I wiped the sweat from my chest, cleared my throat and continued my workout. I found myself daydreaming about his hands touching my stomach, slowly making its way into my pants; replacing his hands with his lips. I could imagine the oral expressions that he could give. "Jesus! Stacie… You don't even know the man, and here you go being a hoe!" These are the types of conversations that I had to have with myself.

I left the gym and didn't return for a few days, but when I did, there he was. The gym was light that day, and there was barely anyone there. As I was walking past the weight room, there he was, shirtless! Everything was perfect. His chest chiseled like Michael Angelo himself carved it, abs that look like a washboard. I almost wanted to take off my soaking, wet panties and wash them across those abs. My eyes stopped right at the top of his gym shorts, which looked like it led to the Garden of Eden!

I snapped myself out of my trance and made a b-line straight for the showers! There was no working out in me on that day. Just looking at him made me cum and I could feel the warm juices, making its way through my panties and on my thighs.

Showered, dressed and heading out the door, when I heard, "Hi." I turned around and there he stood.

Keeping it as cool as I could, I cleared my throat and returned with, "Hello."

"I didn't see you doing your usual thigh master this morning." He was looking at my thighs as he was saying it.

"Well, I have an early class, so I just did one of the Zumba classes in the front." I was simply lying through my teeth.

"Class?"

"Yes, I'm a college student."

"Ah, ok. Well, I don't want you to be late for class, so I'll let you be on your way." I nodded. "I'm Ethan by the way." Extending his hand for me to shake it.

"Stacie." Shaking his hand. "Well, it was nice to meet you, Ethan."

"Likewise. See you around." I smiled and exited the gym.

I was on cloud nine for a few hours. "Lord, if you made his personality like you made his body, you've made perfection, and I want him!" Who talks to God about a man? I do! I had a great day at school that day.

From the first hello, I already had us married, with two kids (a boy and girl), a beautiful house, with a white picket fence and matching cars; very high school, I know, but that's how "girlie" he made me feel. And all the man said was hello! But the reality was, I was a Junior in college, studying to become a Pharmacist and Ethan is a dentist with his own

practice.

# **<u>Chapter 2</u>**

I ran into Ethan a few weeks later at a coffee shop near the gym that we usually do our work out. With my finals coming up soon, I was putting in some major studying and the gym was the last thing on my "to do" list. "Hi, Stacie right."

"Yes, it is. I'm surprised you remembered." I turned my attention from Ethan to place my order with the young lady, standing patiently behind the counter. "Ethan, correct?"

There was that smile, "Yes, I'm surprised you remember. I haven't seen you in here before."

I mumbled to myself, "How could anyone forget?"

"Did you say something?"

Passing the young lady behind the counter my money, I replied, "No. no. I come here sometimes when I'm in need of something strong to keep me up." That's what my mouth said, but inside my head, I was thinking, *that something strong to keep me up, could be you.*

"That's right; you're a college student."

"Yes, I am. That's why I haven't been hitting the gym lately." Before I knew it, the words were already out of my mouth. "I mean, not that you were looking for me or anything."

He smiled, he was too much of a gentleman to laugh. "Stacie, do you have a few minutes to sit and talk?"

"Ummm, sure, I have a few minutes." We went and found an open table and had a seat. "So, Ethan, what do you do?"

"I'm a dentist." I nodded while sipping my coffee. "An adult dentist."

"Is that a hint that I need to come see you?" I asked sarcastically.

# **Chapter 3**

I threw my phone on the couch and started looking around my living room to see if anything was out of place, it wasn't. Let me check the guest bathroom; everything was a go in there as well. Now, what do I do? Oh, call Rosalyn! I grabbed my phone and started dialing. Tapping my foot, praying that she picked up. "Hello." She answered.

"Roz, hey girl." Rosalyn (Roz) was my childhood friend, and we have known each other since Kindergarten. We instantly became friends on the first day of school and have been friends ever since then.

"Don't hey Roz me, whatcha want?" She was a no-nonsense person, and I loved her for that. She was the opposite of me. She was happily married to her college sweetheart, with two beautiful kids that I adored.

"What makes you think that I want something?" I asked, laughing.

"I haven't heard from you in about two weeks, and now you are calling me in your I need a favor voice." I was laughing so hard! "Why are you laughing? I'm not playing." Before long she was laughing herself. "Seriously, what's up girl?"

"Nothing much. I've been in this house for the most part, with my head buried in these books. Just got finished with my finals."

"Oh yeah. How'd you do?"

"As if you have to ask! A's across the board!" Doing my happy dance again.

"Stand yo behind still!" She said laughing.

"How do you know I'm dancing? Still laughing.

"Really? How long have I known you? Well, I'm proud of you."

"Awe, thanks, friend. Ok, listen." I started laughing again.

"I knew it, I knew it! What do you want heffa?" She was laughing just as hard.

"Ok. I met this guy almost a month ago at the gym. Girl, when I say, fine, that's an understatement. Anyway, he asked me out; I declined, because I had to study for finals right. Then I opened my big mouth and told him that I would have drinks with him tonight to unwind from all the studying, but then I came home, got comfortable, didn't feel like going out and invited him over."

"So why are you calling me?"

"Because I don't know him like that and just in case I come up missing, somebody needs to know something. When he gets here, I'm going to take a picture of him and send it to your phone."

"Girl, you are crazy." We were both laughing hysterically.

My doorbell rang and my nerves shot straight to my stomach! It was too late to be scared now. I looked around to make sure that there was nothing out of place, checked my butt in the dress that I had on and proceeded to answer the door.

Ethan arrived with not one, but two bottles of wine in hand. His head tilted to the side, looking like something that stepped straight off the front cover of a magazine. "Hello." I greeted my guest.

"Hi. I didn't know if one bottle would be enough, so I grabbed two. I hope that's ok." He gestured holding a bottle in each hand.

"It's fine. Come in." Nerves still a little shaky, I moved aside and let him in. As he walked in, he leaned in and kissed my cheek. The chemistry between us was off the charts! I began to say a silent prayer in my head: *"Lord, please allow me to behave myself and not allow my vajayjay to do the thinking for me. Amen."*

"Would you like to open a bottle now or wait?"

Without giving it a second thought, I grabbed a bottle out of his hands and said, "Now." I needed something to calm my nerves. This man was fine and was wearing an intoxicating scent that was about to make me jump on him right then and there! "Please, have a seat, wherever you would like. I will open this and grab some glasses."

"Would you like for me to open it?"

"No, I'm good, you're my guest. Allow me to be a gracious hostess." I took both bottles from his hands. "I will be right back. Make yourself comfortable." I placed one bottle in the fridge, grabbed two glasses, popped the cork and began to pour. When I returned to the sitting area, there he sat on the chase. The chase of all places! He knew what he was doing! I cleared my throat as I stood there watching him. "The chase? Really"

All I saw was his teeth. This man was fine, sexy, handsome, and cute, did I miss anything? Lawd! "You said anywhere." I held up a glass and nodded. I didn't sit next to him; I decided to sit on the love seat. I had to at least play a little coy. "You're leaving me over here all by myself?"

I took a sip of wine before I spoke. "For now. So, tell me a little about yourself Ethan; other than the fact that you love to work out." There was that smile again. "And that you have a great smile."

If he were lighter, you would have seen that he was blushing. "Well, I'm forty, divorced and that great smile that you speak about is all because I'm a dentist."

"I remember you saying that you were a dentist the day that we had coffee. Really? I would have never guessed."

Taking a sip from his glass. "Really what?"

"You said that you were forty, I would have never guessed that." My glass was almost empty.

"Ah. Most people say that they would have never guessed that I was divorced." Taking a huge gulp from his glass. "Can I get you some more wine?"

I looked down, "I didn't realize that it was almost empty. No, let me." Reaching for his glass as well. Returning with both glasses topped off, "Here you are."

"Thank you." We both sipped at the same time. I wonder if he was just as nervous as I was. "So, tell me about Stacie, other than you're a student."

"I'm a student as you know; this is my junior year. Just finished my finals, so I guess you can say that I'm a senior."

"What are you studying? Both of our glasses were damn near empty again. He looked at his glass and mine, "We are really going through this wine, aren't we?"

Nodding my head, "Yeah, I guess we are, and I'm studying to become a pharmacist." Reaching for his glass to top it off, once more. When I returned from the kitchen, Ethan had repositioned himself on the loveseat where I was. I didn't say a word; I just handed him his glass.

"I have a confession."

"Oh yeah, what's that?" I asked.

"I was a little bit nervous about coming over. I know that I was the one that hinted about it in the first place, but that was because you didn't seem like you were interested in going out with me."

I laughed, "Why do you think I've been throwing these glasses back so fast?" He joined me in laughter. "I'm nervous as well. It's not that I didn't want to go out with you, but I really did have a long day with finals, and I just wanted to relax."

"I can help you with that if you would like." I gave him the side eye. He noticed and began to laugh. "Not like that, just a shoulder massage. Is that ok? Nothing is going to happen that you don't want to happen."

I took a few more sips from my glass, stood up, opened his legs and sat down between them. He began to massage my neck, and I'm telling you, that was it. Stacie went away, and my vajayjay started doing all the thinking! I closed my eyes, leaned my head back a little and enjoyed the moment. His hands move from my shoulders to my neck, down my arms and back up to my neck. I let out a little moan, and before I knew it, I felt his lips on mine. I didn't stop him, because I wanted it, just as much as he did.

Finally, we stopped. My head was spinning, my body had chills, and I was wet and ready! I didn't say anything about the way that I was feeling, I stood up, retrieved my glass from the table and downed what was left. "My glass is empty; I'm going to go open the other bottle." I left him sitting on the couch and went to the kitchen. I began to open the other bottle of wine, thinking to myself, if he kisses me like that again, it's on!

I suddenly realized that I didn't ask Ethan if he needed or wanted more wine. As I turned to walk back into the sitting area, there he stood in my kitchen. "I realized that I didn't ask if you wanted or needed more wine." As I was holding the wine bottle in my hand, he walked over to me, took the wine bottle from my hand, sat it on the counter and began kissing me again. My entire body was on fire! I tried to speak between kisses, but couldn't get a word in. I pulled back from him.

"I'm sorry," he said. I just thought you felt what I did.

"You don't have to apologize; we are both adults; consenting adults and yes, I felt what you did."

"Then why did you pull away?" Walking towards me.

"I really don't know." He started softly kissing my hands, my neck, my forehead and then my ears. I let out another moan.

"That sound tells me that you don't want me to stop. Do you?"

"No, I don't."

"Good." One, quick, forceful turn, I was bent over my stove. Again, my body felt a rush of adrenaline, mixed with a cool sensation at the same time. He lifted my dress above my waist and kicked my legs open. "No panties."

"No." Nothing else was said. In my kitchen, dinner was being served, and my stove was never turned on! This man's lips were soft! He was on his knees, devouring my pussy like it was his last meal. I had no complaints! He ate for what seemed like hours, when I reached the ultimate point of ecstasy, I damn near fainted. In all my thirty-two years of living, I have never had such an intense orgasm.

He caught my limp body, laid me down gently on the floor, kissed my stomach, made his way to my breast, then my neck, and finally landed on my ears. He whispered, "Should I continue?" I was so weak, and all I could do was shake my head, indicating a yes. There was a short pause as he placed a condom on his well-erected dick. He was serving everything that he had in my kitchen, and he was serving it exactly the way that I wanted it. Hard and a little rough. This man was blessed, in more ways than one!

There was not one thing that he didn't do right. Every stroke, every wine, every thrust, brought nothing put pleasure. He had my hands stretched above my head, pouring everything that he had into me. I moaned, bit my lip and said *Oh God* too many times to count. He was man-handling me, and this was the one time that I didn't mind at all. He now had me on my knees, with my ass, high in the air. He went so deep at one point; I could feel him in my stomach. With every thrust he threw, I threw it back at him. Whatever direction of a whine, he went, I whined with him. We were in synch. After a while, I heard little whispers, "Stacie, Stacie, Stacie." There was no need for me to answer, I knew why he was calling my name. Before long, he said, "Oh shit! Ahh, shit," and fell on my back.

I slid down to the floor to give my knees a break; he didn't move, he just laid there on my back. He finally spoke, "So you're not a light-weight."

"What? What does that mean?"

"You can hold your own."

I turned over to face him. He never moved, now he was laying on my stomach. "Did you think that I would be a light-weight?" I said it with a bit of an attitude.

"I didn't mean it like that. Don't get salty." I pushed his head off me and got up. "What's wrong? What did I say?" Asking questions as he was getting up off the floor.

"Did you size me from the moment that you met me?" Pulling out cleaning supplies from under the kitchen sink. I clean when I'm aggravated or pissed.

"No! You have a small frame, and you took everything that I gave, that's all I meant by that." He was pulling up his pants at this point. "Really Stacie, are you about to clean? Right now?" Grabbing my hands, pulling me towards him.

"Yes. I clean when I'm aggravated." He laughed. "What's funny?" I was pulling away from him. He grabbed me around my waist and pulled me back to him.

"I'm sorry, I didn't mean to aggravate you. I didn't mean anything by it. You're a little feisty I see." I was still trying to pull myself away from him. He started kissing my neck, "Stop it, just less than five minutes ago, you were smiling from ear to ear. Now, look at you. You're cute when you're mad."

I started blushing. "Don't try to talk your way out of this." He was right though, five minutes ago, I was in Heaven. He kissed, kissed and kissed some more. His lips felt like cotton. Ok, I was done being "salty." "You're right; but don't ever size me again like I'm short."

"Well, you are kinda short," he said laughing. I pushed my butt against his pelvis, and he let me go. "You are something else, but I like it." He finished putting himself together, and we walked back to the sitting area. We talked a little more and time got away from us. I decided that it was getting late and that he should go because he had to work the next morning. "Ok, I'll go, can we have lunch tomorrow?"

"Umm, I don't know. I have a few things that I need to take care of." I was lying; I just didn't want him to think that I was readily available whenever he wanted me to be.

"Ok. Well, let me know when you're free."

"Fair enough." I walked him to the door. We kissed a little before I opened the door. "Good night."

# **<u>Chapter 4</u>**

Graduation was here! I made it! I received my white coat and was now a certified pharmacist. Ethan and I had been dating for a year at this point, and there he sat in the audience with my mom as I walked across the stage and received my degree. My father passed away during my senior year in high school. My mother and I wanted for nothing. It seemed as if life was good. There was only one thing that I was holding on to, that I wasn't quite sure how to tell Ethan. In time, I kept telling myself.

My father left me a very hefty inheritance, but money didn't heal the hurt that I felt when he died. My father provided well for my mother and I, but he died with a secret that we found out the day of his funeral. My father had another daughter. She was older than I was; he had her before he married my mother, but never told her about it. He was secretly taking care of her and visited her often, but we never knew. Needless to say, we were shocked.

I was angry; my mother wanted to get to know this girl, but I didn't. At the funeral when she walked up to us and said, "Hi, I'm Sylvester's daughter." I called her a liar and ran out! How could she come to my father's funeral and make such a crazy accusation? I lived with my father all my life, and there was never a clue that he had another daughter. My mother, on the other hand, believed her. She said there was something about the young lady and the way that my father acted lead her to believe the young lady. She often tried to talk to me about her, but I didn't want to hear it. I didn't even want to know her name, and I never did.

That wasn't my secret; it was my father's. The death of my father and then this other daughter did something to me.

I acted out; I became very promiscuous. My mother knew that something was going on with me, but she just wasn't sure what it was. The day that I graduated from high school, I moved out and bought a condo. My mother wasn't happy with my decision, but I knew that I couldn't keep "handling business" and living with her. Having my own place would give me much needed freedom to do what I wanted to do. I didn't want anything; I had no business doing any of those things that I was doing. Going to college was the furthest thing from my mind.

I started having sex, and I enjoyed it, so I decided to make money doing it. I was a high-end escort. I didn't need the money, but why not make money if I was going to be laying on my back? Why did I need a four-year degree to work for someone else? I made more than enough money, being the trophy piece on the arm of some rich fool that paid girls to hang out and sleep with them. I also had the money that my dad left me that I had yet to touch. If my mother knew, she would be mortified.

From age eighteen to twenty-nine, I lived this life, not having a care in the world. Sleeping all day and being up half the night, taking trips that were paid for by doctors, lawyers, judges, etc. I was living a semi-dangerous life style, but it didn't matter at the time. I never wanted a relationship. If my father could be married to my mother all those years and keep such a big secret from her, why would I want that? I didn't and did everything that I could to stay away from a relationship, until I met Ethan.

Just out of the blue one day, I decided that was no longer how I wanted to live. I wanted more out of life. I will never forget the day that I told my mother that I was going to college. You would have thought that she won the lottery.

Every now and then, I would drift into being an escort, but it wasn't like it was before. If one of my old clients called and were in a jam, I helped them out. After meeting Ethan, I did it less and less, but I never completely stopped, but I knew that I had to.

The ceremony was over, and there the two loves of my lives were beaming with pride. We went out for dinner later that night, and I ran into one of my old clients. Of course, we acted as if we didn't know each other because that lifestyle was all about privacy. All through dinner, my phone would not stop buzzing. It was the client that I ran into (Mr. Kelly by name). He needed an escort for an event that he had coming up out of town the following week and wanted me to attend. I did my best to ignore my phone, but my mom had to make mention of it. "Do people not know you're out celebrating?" she asked.

"It's just classmates that's trying to see what I'm doing tonight. Many of them are having parties and are trying to see if I wanted to attend."

"Do you want to?" Ethan chimed in. My mother was looking at me to see what my response would be.

"No. I'm fine right where I am. I will just turn my phone off."

"Are you sure baby? I understand if you do."

"Ethan, I'm sure." Before I turned my phone off, I sent him a quick text. *Why are you trying to get rid of me? Do you not want to take me back to your place and give me proper congratulations? Fuck the shit out of me?"* His phone buzzed, he took it out of his pocket, read my message, smiled and nodded his head. After dinner, we dropped my mother off at home and went to his house. "Now, why were you trying to get rid of me?"

"I wasn't babe; I just understand that today was a big deal for you and you may have wanted to let your hair down and celebrate with your friends." I pulled my hair down and tossed it around. He just laughed. I reached over, unzipped his pants, pulled his dick out and sucked it all the way to his place. "Stacie." I didn't reply. "Stacie, you're gonna make me wreck this truck." I held my head up, gave him a look, and he held it on the road. We pulled into the garage, and he pushed the seat back. I climbed on top and made love to my man. "You are something else; you know that."

"Isn't that what you like about me?"

"Among other things." We walked into the house, there was music playing, candles everywhere, and wine chilling.

I was surprised' I had no clue. He wasn't trying to rush home as if he had something planned. "What is all this? When did you have time?"

"I have ways of getting things done that I need to get done." He pulled me towards the blanket that he had laid out on the floor. "I love you, Stacie Lee." It was the first time that he ever said those words to me. I was in total awe and scared at the same time.

"Ethan.....I don't know what to say."

"I was hoping that you would say that you loved me too." With a look of disappointment on his face.

"Oh baby, I do. I love you, Ethan." When the words exited my mouth, he was holding a tiny, silver box in his hand. "What is this?"

"I love you Stacie. Will you marry me?" I jumped up so fast; I scared myself.

"I, I, I can't." The thought of me being an escort came rushing in like a flood.

He closed the box, scratched his head and asked, "Why?"

"I just can't."

"That's not a good enough reason Stacie. You just told me that you loved me, or did you say it because I did."

I turned to face him, "Ethan, I do love you. I just have some things that I need to work out."

"Am I missing something here? We've been dating a little over a year; you just graduated, so I know that's not it. You already have a job lined up, so that's not it. We damn near live together, so that couldn't be it. What is it Stacie?"

I was wringing my hands so hard, I thought that I was going to twist them off. "I just need some time."

"This is bullshit."

"You're already established Ethan; I'm just starting. You've done the marriage thing before, I haven't, and I honestly don't know if I ever want to."

"Why have you never said anything before?"

"It never came up. Look, baby I'm sorry." I was reluctant to tell him about my father, but I had to say something. "My father and mother were married for twenty years."

"Ok. That's a long time, that's a good thing."

I was pacing. "On the day of my father's funeral, my mother and I found out that he had another daughter."

"What?!"

"Yeah, that's the reaction that I had. That moment took away everything that I knew was the truth about him. I didn't understand how he could have kept that secret for so long from the people that he claimed that he loved. That messed me up.

I did some things that I'm not proud of, and that's why I started college so late."

"Do you have a relationship with her?"

"Sad to say that I don't. I ran out of the funeral home when she introduced herself. My mother has been in contact with her, but I never cared to know the details."

"Ok, but why should that stop you from marrying me?"

"I don't trust marriage. We are fine, just the way we are."

"Stacie, I want a wife, children, a family."

"So, what are you saying? If I don't want to marry you, then we are over?"

"I don't want that. I want you to say that you'll marry me. We don't have to get married right away. We can give it some time so that you can work through why you don't trust marriage."

"Why can't we just continue our relationship the way that it is while I work through it?" he reluctantly put the ring back in the box. A small part of me was relieved. "It's beautiful, for what it's worth."

"It would be more beautiful on your finger."

I hung my head down. "I'm sorry baby. I really am."

He walked over to console me, let out a loud sigh, "It's ok babe. It's ok. We will revisit this topic another time. Is there anything else that I need to know?"

This would have been the perfect time to tell him about me being an escort, but I lied. "No, there's nothing else."

Morning could not come fast enough! I needed my best friend, and I needed her now! Ethan left for work, and I was on the phone as soon as I heard the garage door go down. "Yes ma'am," Rosalyn answered.

"Girl! Ethan asked me to marry him."

Screaming, "When is the wedding?! I'm ready; this is going to be awesome!" She was just rambling away.

"Pump ya breaks friend. Pump ya breaks."

"Why?! What did you do?"

"What makes you think that it was me?"

"Number one, he asked you, so it couldn't be him. Number two, I know you. So, what's the problem?"

"Before we get into that, why weren't you at my graduation yesterday?"

"The twins were running a fever. You didn't want the crying and teething of a little one-year old's there with all that noise."

"Because it was my babies, you're forgiven."

"Don't try to change the subject, why is there not going to be a wedding?"

"Roz, you know my past, and I just don't know how to tell him or if he'll be accepting of it."

"Hiding it from him isn't going to help. That's your past; you were young. I'm sure he will understand."

"Wellll."

"Well, what?!"

"I have been doing a little escorting off and on for a few loyal clients, but only for out of town trips and there is no sex involved."

"If I were near you, I would slap you! Stacie, what are you doing? You need to get that mess out and now!"

"I know. I know. Last night I ran into one of them while we were at dinner and he kept texting my phone about going out of town with him."

"I would hope that you said no."

"I haven't said anything. I turned my phone off during dinner and when we got to Ethan's house, was when he popped the question."

"But you're going to say no or ignore it all together, right?"

"Wellll."

"Bring yo ass over to my house, now! So that I can punch you in yo face!" Roz was my girl for sure. She gave it to me straight, no matter how much I disliked it. When I first told her about escorting, she disagreed with me, gave me her opinion, but she never once judged me.

"You're so violent. This guy is a very loyal client; I never have to spend more than two hours at whatever event that he goes to. It's out of town, nobody will ever know, and this will be my last time. I promise."

"I never understood why you started escorting in the first place, but I guess it wasn't for me to understand. I don't agree with it, but you're going to do what you wanna do anyway. You need to tell Ethan, before this backfires in your face."

"It won't."

"If you say so. I gotta go, girl. Call me later."

"I will. Bye."

# **Chapter 5**

I was trying to think of a good reason to give Ethan as to why I would be out of town that night. I couldn't think of anything. I had been racking my brain for a week. This was my last escort, and I made that perfectly clear to all my clients that I was randomly doing jobs for. My phone started ringing and interrupted my thoughts. "Hello."

"Hey, babe. I just got an email about a last-minute conference that I must attend tomorrow night."

No excuse needed! He just gave me one. "Oh, ok. How long will you be gone?"

"A day or two. Are you ok with that?"

"It's work Ethan; I have no choice but to be ok with it."

"Did you have anything planned for us?"

"No, I didn't. I was going to meet up with some old friends' tomorrow night anyway, so this works out perfectly."

"Ok. Will I see you tonight?"

"I think I'm going to stay at home tonight, finish some projects that I've been working on." Though I graduated and became a pharmacist, my passion was writing, so I started some online classes in journalism and got a part-time job at our local paper.

"Do you want me to come over?"

"If you do, I won't get anything done, and you know it."

"You're letting your man go out of town without getting any?" I could see the smirk on his face.

"Babe. Really? We have sex damn near every night. A day or two isn't going to kill you."

"Yes, I know, and that's why I want some tonight because I'm going to be without it for two days."

"I didn't think about it like that. How many more patients do you have?"

I could hear him, clicking his computer, "I have four."

"No breaks in between?"

"I know my baby, what are you thinking?"

"I can come to your office and give you a little afternoon delight." I was trying anything not to spend the night. I needed to prepare for this job and get my mind right, but Ethan wasn't having it.

"That sounds good, but will I get more tonight? Two days Stacie, two days." *DR. Hamilton, your twelve o'clock is here.* His assistant interrupted.

"I will leave work early, go home and try to finish some of my projects and I will see you tonight." I could see that silly smile on his face, whenever he got his way.

"Ok baby. I love you."

"Love you too." I kicked the floor. A pharmacist with a wild side. I had to do better. "This was my last job" is what I kept telling myself. I should have tried to talk myself out of it, instead of into it. I did love Ethan, and I knew that I had to cut all ties with this escort business and tell him. I didn't know what the outcome would be. I was afraid of what the outcome would be, but I had to be honest with him.

Instead of staying in, I decided to make dinner reservations at his favorite restaurant. I thought about getting him drunk, but that was a bad idea. I would get absolutely no sleep. *"Hey, I made reservations for seven at Blue Tavern. I will meet you there."*

*"Ok, see you at seven."*

About an hour later, there was a knock at the door; a flower delivery. The card read, *"I've never been away from you, and I miss you already. I love you, Stacie."* I felt horrible! I had to call this thing off. As soon as I left work, I was calling this guy and have him find someone else to escort him. I couldn't do this to Ethan anymore; I couldn't risk it. Better yet, I was calling him now.

"Hi, Mr. Kelly, it's Stacie. Listen, I don't think that I will able to escort you tomorrow night."

"Hello, Stacie. Why not? It's really last minute and it's going to be kind of hard to find someone else as beautiful and professional as you are." Mr. Kelly was a very prominent businessman who believed in being very discreet. I could understand why he wasn't married though. He was very demanding and a little pompous. I only had to deal with him for a very short period of time, and I was getting paid.

"Right. I understand, but I really have gotten out of the business. I just do it for a few high-end clients like yourself from time to time, but since I've graduated, I'm getting out of the business altogether."

"I do understand Miss Lee; however, will you just oblige me once more. This meeting is very important to me."

The phone was silent. "I tell you what, to prove to you how important this is to me, I will double your pay."

"Are you serious? Just for a few hours?"

"Yes, ma'am."

I wasn't really pressed for the cash, but what the heck. This was my absolute last escorting job. "This must be really important. Ok, but let's be clear, this is my absolute last job."

"Understood. See you tomorrow." The phone went silent. All I had to do was get through tonight without guilt eating me alive and then tomorrow night, and I would be home free.

The pharmacy was hell today! I was so busy that I lost track of time and was running late for dinner with Ethan. I rushed out the door and gave him a call in the car, "Hey babe, work has been hell today, I'm running a little late, I'll be there as soon as I can." I left a message. There would be no time for me to drive home, shower, change clothes and make it to the restaurant anywhere near time. I had to think of something and fast. I can't possibly show up looking and smelling like "all day." Thank God, I kept Summer's Eve wipes in my purse. I could stop by my favorite store, grab something to change into and freshen up in the bathroom. That's exactly what I did! I was only ten minutes late.

Ethan spotted me before I did. There he stood, fine as always. I loved this man! I couldn't wait to get away from the lies that I've been telling all these years; even the ones that I've been telling myself. Greeting him with a kiss, "Sorry I'm late."

"I'll wait for you anywhere." He had a different look in his eyes tonight; his eyes were as bright as his smile.

I kissed him again. "You are so sweet; I love you."

"You are so beautiful."

"Thank you, baby. I am enjoying all the compliments, but what's going on with you tonight?"

"Don't I always compliment you?"

"Indeed, you do, but something is different tonight. Your eyes are different."

"You make me happy Stacie. I love you, I want to spend the rest of my life with you."

"Baby. We will. We are."

Before I knew it, a small, black box sat in front of me. "So, say that you'll marry me."

I covered my face to try and stop the tears from falling. Mumbling through my covered lips, "Ethan, we've talked about this." I fumbled with the box.

"You also said that we would revisit the conversation." He touched my hands and said, "I'm revisiting the conversation."

"Why here? Why now? I mean baby, you're putting me on the spot."

"Did you not just tell me that you loved me? Don't you want to spend the rest of your life with me, have a few little Ethan's? What's the problem, Stacie?"

"You know that I love you, and you also know my reluctance about getting married. Can we talk about this when we get home?"

"Sure. Whatever you want. It's always Stacie's way, right?"

"That's not fair. You just sprung this on me." He didn't say anything; he was just staring at his menu. "So, you aren't talking to me?"

Without looking up, he replied, "Let's just get through dinner."

I placed the ring in front of him, gathered my purse and left. He didn't try to stop me, nor did he follow me. I didn't hear from him the rest of the night or the next morning. I knew he was upset; we never went a day without at least texting each other. I could not fully give myself to this man until I tied up all my loose ends.

I prepared myself to escort Mr. Kelly to whatever business meeting that he had to attend. I had no idea what the man did for a living; I was merely eye candy. I drove the two hours out of town to meet Mr. Kelly. It was unusual that he asked me to meet him in his hotel lobby. We always meet outside of wherever he was staying. "Why are we meeting in your hotel lobby?" I asked as I approached Mr. Kelly.

He flashed a very charming smile, hugged me as if I were truly his lover and whispered, "Because this is where my meeting is."

I smiled awkwardly and embraced him. I wasn't too sure about this. "Mr. Kelly, you are aware that I am not sleeping with you?"

"Oh dear, relax. They have a very nice bar and restaurant inside. It didn't make sense to go elsewhere when you have the best right in front of you." He gestured for me to walk inside. The hotel was indeed beautiful. What did I expect? Mr. Kelly always took me to the finest of everything. We sat at the bar, had a few drinks, did the idle chit-chat and waited for his guest to arrive. "There he is."

I stood, turned to greet his guest and thought that I was seeing things. My glass fell from my hands because I was so numb. There he stood, the man that I loved! Ethan! He was equally shocked. I couldn't even open my mouth to say anything.

He looked at me dazed and confused for a moment. I think we both forgot that Mr. Kelly was even there. "Stacie! What the hell are you doing here?" He didn't give me a chance to respond before he went on to the next question. "I thought you were hanging out with friends tonight. What happened to that? Say something!"

"You aren't giving me a chance!" I said, with tears rolling down my face.

Mr. Kelly chimed in, "I guess that the two of you know each other?"

"Know each other! Stacie Lee, a pharmacist that left me sitting at a table in a restaurant last night, because I asked her to marry me. So yes, it's safe to say that we know each other. But I can see now why I could never get a yes out of her." I just stood there tears still rolling. I couldn't say anything; I didn't know where to start. "I'm waiting, baby. I'm waiting for you to explain to me why you are here, two hours from home at my business meeting. Answer me, Stacie! I flinched, I had never heard Ethan raise his voice, but he had a good reason to do so.

All I could mumble was, "I'm sorry."

"That's not an explanation Stacie." He then turned to Mr. Kelly, "I'm sorry, but is there any possible way that we can reschedule this meeting?" Mr. Kelly picked up his drink from the table, drank what was left in the glass and exited the bar. He turned back to me, "I'm still waiting Stacie."

"Can we talk about this somewhere else?" He was furious with me and had every right to be. "Please?" We exited the bar, walked out through the front and waited for the valet to get our cars. I was still crying.

Trying not to make a bigger scene than he already had, he tried to calmly talk to me. "Again, what are you doing here? What is going on? How do you even know Mr. Kelly?

I had no other choice, I had to tell him the truth. Wiping the tears from my face, I softly said, "I'm an escort."

"What did you say? I don't think that I heard you right."

I stood upright, wiping the remaining tears from my face, cleared my throat and repeated myself, "I'm an escort."

He did a little nervous laugh and said, "You have got to be fucking kidding me. I must be getting punked!" He started looking around for cameras.

"I haven't done it in a while. I was young and messed up when I got into it and when I started school, it helped with expenses. When we met, I was breaking away from it, tonight, was going to be my last job." I started crying again, a little harder.

"Was going to be?!"

"It is my last job. I tried to get out of it, but he said that it was too late for him to find someone else."

"Don't give me that bullshit, Stacie! If you didn't want to be here, you shouldn't have been here!"

"Ethan, please, calm down." There were people coming in and out of the restaurant, and they were starting to stare.

"Calm down! So, this is why you wouldn't marry me? This is why you walked out on me last night? So that you could come and fuck some motherfucker you're escorting?! So basically, you're a high-end prostitute?

"No! I wasn't going to sleep with him! I've never slept with him or anyone else!" Valet had brought our cars to the front.

I was reaching for my car door, "So you're just going to leave like this?"

"Ethan, what do you want me to do?"

"I want you to talk to me. Make me understand this shit! I've asked you to marry me, not once, but twice. You turned me down both times, and now I'm standing here looking and feeling like a fool!

The look in his eyes made me feel worse, every word he spoke, pierced my heart. I hurt him, and that was never my intention, it's what I was trying to avoid. I didn't know how to make it right. "Ethan, get in your car, I will call you, and we can talk on the way home."

He wiped the few tears that he was starting to shed, jumped in his car and drove off. I got in my car and followed him. I was now in my safe haven, and I let out the loudest scream that I could. He looked at me as if he didn't know me, the disappointment that I saw in his eyes was unbearable. I tried to get myself together as much as I could before I called him. It wasn't working. I called his phone several times, but he would not pick up. The last time that I called, it went straight to voicemail. I was hitting my steering wheel and screaming at the top of my lungs. The one thing that I was trying to avoid happened; my LIES caught up with me, and there was nothing that I could do to.

I tried calling his phone once more; I got the same results. I drove the rest of the way home in silence, trying to figure out what I could say or do to make Ethan understand that I was truly sorry and that I loved him. I didn't want to lose him, but it looked as if I already had.

# **<u>Chapter 6</u>**

A few weeks had gone by, and I'm yet to hear from Ethan. I called, he wouldn't answer or return my calls. Texted, no response. I even tried emailing him, no response, and he even stopped coming to the gym. I was sure that I had lost him.

I couldn't take it anymore; he had to hear me out. I was scared shitless, but I was going to take my chances and just show up at his house. After work, I turned my car down his street and couldn't bring myself to stop, so I drove home. I got home, piddled around my house for a little while and decided to give Ethan a call. As always, no answer. I had to call Roz.

"Yes, ma'am." She answered.

Sniffling, I uttered, "He won't answer the phone, he won't reply to any of my text or my emails. I thought about going to his house, but I couldn't bring myself to stop."

"Aww Stacie, honey, I'm sorry. I'm sure he will come around."

"No, he won't. You should have seen the look on his face, Roz. It's like I was a stranger to him."

"I know that it hurts, but he caught you Stacie, and it's not like you came out and told him. Just give him some time." That was Roz, the straight shooter. "I wanted to slap you when you told me that you were going to do this last job. I'm sorry that you are going through this, but I love you enough to tell you the truth."

"I know. I know." Still sobbing.

"He's just hurt right now. He needs time to process everything that he knows thus far. He will come around, trust me. That man loves you."

I interrupted, "Loved."

"No, he loves you. He asked you to marry him twice. You can't make me believe that within a few weeks that the love has totally disappeared. If that's the case, he never loved you at all."

"I guess you're right. I just wish that he would say something, anything."

"Put yourself in his shoe baby-girl. Examine your feelings and tell me what you come up with. I love you; I have to go. Talk to you soon."

"Thanks for listening. Love you too. Kiss the babies for me." I didn't know what I was going to do with myself for the rest of the day. I had some writing that I could catch up on, as well as some lingering homework that I could complete. Laundry that I could do, ok, let me get moving. Before I knew it, it was eleven o'clock. Time flew by fast, and I didn't think about Ethan once.

I headed for the shower to prepare myself for the next day, Ethan was back on my mind. The more I thought about it, the angrier I got. Yes, I was wrong, but he was going to hear me out. I stepped out of the shower, threw on a dress and headed to his house. There I was, standing at his door at midnight and he answered. I had no idea what I was going to say, but I was happy that he opened the door. The crisp, night air, made my nipples stand at attention through the sheer, white, dress that I was wearing. He pulled me inside and greeted me with a kiss. I melted.

The door closed behind us; he firmly grabbed my ass, and the kisses became more intense. "I've missed you." He mumbled through kisses. My lips said nothing, but my eyes and body said everything. His touch was so soft, he smelled so good, and I was taking it all in. My body began to get chills.

He slipped my dress off, admiring my silk, soft, voluptuous curves. I was wearing nothing underneath. He kissed my forehead and made his way down to my neck, to my perky, erect breast, then to my stomach, until he reached the sweet taste of honey that laid between my thick thighs.

As soon as his lips touched it, I let out a moan. I missed this man and the amazing sex! He looked up at me, and I caught his glance. It seemed as if we could read each other's souls. I kneeled in front of him, embraced him as tears began to roll down my face, wrapping my arms around his neck. "Baby, I'm sorry." I kept repeating myself because I didn't know what else to say. "I won't ever hurt you again, will you please forgive me? That was a part of my past and I should have let it stay there. I love you, Ethan."

"I love you too, Stacie. I just didn't know how to take that. I still don't really know how to take it. I've been trying to process it over and over in my head, and I just don't understand. Escorting is not something that you had to do. Your dad made sure that you and your mom were well taken care of, like what were you thinking?" His tone went from soft to a little aggressive.

"Ethan, I was young. My mother doesn't even know about this. It wasn't something that I had to do; I admit to that but it's something that had happened, and I can't change it. I can't say that I'm sorry enough, but that's something that's in my past."

He got up off the floor and turned away from me. "Stacie, the past was a few years ago, this was just a month or two ago. I would hardly call that your past."

"I was doing a favor for an old client, that's all that was. I swear." I got up, walked over to him and wrapped my arms around his waist. "Baby, please, I need you to forgive me. I love you, that's why I didn't accept your marriage proposals. I wanted to make sure that all this was cleared up."

"You hurt me, Stacie. Why weren't you just honest with me from the start?"

"Because I was afraid that I was going to lose you. I didn't want my past to interfere with my future. Baby, I love you. What else can I say? What else can I do?"

He turned around to face me, kissed me on my forehead and led me to the couch. We sat and talked for hours. I explained everything to the best of my ability, not leaving out any details. I didn't want him to feel as if I were lying to him again. I lost his trust, and I knew that it was going to take a lot of work to regain it and I was willing. The sun was coming up, and we were going down. We both played hooky from work that day. We spent the day, getting to know each other, starting over.

A few months had passed, and Ethan and I were getting back into the groove of things. It wasn't easy, but we made it work. I was thankful that I didn't lose a guy that loved me beyond words, forgave me for my lies and embraced my flaws. I messed up, and I was thankful for his forgiveness. Truth be told, if the shoe were on the other foot, would I be as forgiving? He's yet to propose to me again, and that was fine with me. I liked our life just the way it was. Ethan's business was thriving. I also completed my journalism classes and was now the pharmacy manager at my store. Things were good, life was good.

I was now trying to decide if I wanted to continue being a pharmacist full time or start writing more for the paper; I loved writing. Each story brought out something different in me, and I loved it! It seemed as if I were more relaxed and I had more passion when I was writing. Don't get me wrong, I enjoyed being a pharmacist because I loved helping people, but there were times that it could be overwhelming. Until I became more established at the paper, I think I better stick it out with the pharmacy. All I needed was one big breakthrough!

Something huge that would get me noticed, so that I could add

Editor in Chief to my title. Until then…

*The Walberg's*

# <u>Chapter 1</u>

Mark and Tammy Walberg had been married for a little over five years, from the outside looking in; you would think that they had it all together.  Two beautiful girls, good jobs, they lived in a middle-class, upscale neighborhood and whenever they were out in public, they always "looked" the part.  They seemed like the perfect couple, the perfect family, but what LIES beneath.  Hold onto your seats and get ready for the ride!

Marks walks in and slams the door behind him.  Tammy doesn't say a word; she just rolls her eyes and ushers the girls to their rooms. "Mommy, what's wrong with dad?  Is he ok?"  One of the daughters asked.

"I'm sure he's fine baby, he's probably upset about something that had happened at work." Tammy knew better; she and Mark had been arguing all week, but they never argued in front of the girls. She turned the TV on for the girls before going back downstairs to confront Mark. "What's the problem today? Your hoe at work didn't give you any at lunch?"

"No, my hoe at home hasn't given me any all week. I'm sure she's saving it for when her out of town dude comes in." It was sad to say, but truth be told, they both were cheating.

*Laughing*…. "So, I'm the hoe? I'm not the one who has his office buzzing about being caught with his pants down in the men's room with his co-worker, and you expect me to have sex with you?! No way in hell!"

"Tammy, that was months ago! When are you going to let that go?"

"When you stop screwing her! I came by your office two days this week, where were you? And before you decide to lie, you already know that I never ask a question that I don't already know the answer to."

"Then you tell me where I was since you know every damn thing." Tammy wanted to slap him!

"Bitch don't play with me! I know that you and ya bitch took two vacation days off from work! You left here like you were going to work every fucking day, but drove straight to the Motel 6! She's a cheap bitch at that!"

"And where do you go to meet your dude? You think that I don't know that you're sleeping with someone because you damn sure not sleeping with me! Once a month, you always have to work late or hang with the girls. You really think that I'm that stupid?"

"You're right! I am sleeping with someone!" Before Tammy could get another word out of her mouth, Mark slapped her, and she fell to the floor. Holding her face, she looked towards the stairs to make sure that the kids didn't come out of their room. Mark just stood there, with no remorse. Tammy stood up, still holding her face and continued what she was saying: "As I was saying, you're right, I am sleeping with someone, I see him more than once a month, I see him daily.

You ready to hit me again? Trust me you are going to pay for that." Mark knew that she meant what she said. "I'm sick of pretending that we live a perfect life and putting on for our family and friends. I'm sick of hearing my husband's name in the streets, but smiling my way through. I'm sick of it! So yes, I started seeing someone! I got sick of looking like a fool, at least I'm discreet about it."

"So that makes it better because nobody sees you or knows about it? I know about it!"

"Nigga, you don't matter. I'm supposed to care that you know?! Did I know that you were sleeping with someone else? No! If it weren't for my girls, I would have been out of here a long time ago. You're a sorry excuse for a husband, but they love their sorry ass daddy."

"Well, at least we both know why we are still here. I'm going out."

"You need not come back here tonight if you want to live," Mark smirked and walked out. "Bastard." That was the first time that Mark had ever hit Tammy, though he came close a couple of times. She began to cry, still rubbing her face, trying to figure out where their marriage went wrong. They were so happy in the beginning; it was like Mark woke up one day and lost interest in Tammy. Mark didn't return home that night, and that was fine with Tammy. Still feeling the sting on her face, she wanted to kill him.

# **Chapter 2**

Months went by, Mark and Tammy were basically living like roommates for the sake of the children. Mark started staying out more and more. Tammy had to keep coming up with excuses to tell the children as to why daddy wasn't at home. "Daddy is up for a promotion at work sweetie, so he has to work longer hours and take a lot more trips. He will make it up to you." Tammy was sick of lying to the kids, and something had to give way. Tammy was tired of hearing about who Mark was sleeping with and decided to see for herself.

The next morning after dropping the kids off at school, and running a few errands, Tammy decided to pay her husband a visit to his office for lunch. To her surprise, his assistant was sitting at her desk, yet she was startled to see Tammy standing before her. "Tammy, what a pleasant surprise. How are you?"

"It's Mrs. Walberg to you. Would you let my husband know that I'm here?" Tammy replied with a sheepish grin on her face.

"Well, Mrs. Walberg, Mr. Walberg is in a meeting. Shall I tell him that you stopped by?" Returning her response with an equally sheepish grin.

Tammy tilted her head to the side. "If he's in a meeting, why aren't you? You're his assistant."

"Correct, I'm his assistant, not his shadow." This bitch was getting beside herself. Little did she know that Tammy was a little rough around the edges and would drag her up and through this office.

Letting out a little giggle, Tammy replied, "Just let my husband know that I stopped by." Walking away, Tammy began to think. They must think that I'm stupid, Mark was up to something and she was going to find out exactly what it was. It's his lunch hour, and he's in a meeting? That's bull! But why wasn't his lil side piece with him? Walking back to the elevator, Tammy heard Mark's laughter coming from another colleague's office. She walked towards where she heard the laugh coming from, and she didn't knock; she just stood there and listened for a while. There was a lot of whispering, and then snickering. Finally, she knocked. The voices stopped, and there was a lot of rapid movement. "Mark! Open this door! I know you're in there!"

A voice answered with, "One moment please." Looking dazed and confused, Tammy couldn't believe the voice she just heard.

She started talking to herself and beating on the door at the same time, "I know like hell I didn't hear what I think I just heard! Mark! Open it now before I tear this bitch off the hinges!"

Mark opened the door, looking disheveled and nervous. "Tammy, why are you making a scene at my place of employment?! What are you doing here? What do you want?"

Tammy didn't say a word; she pushed passed Mark so that she could lay eyes on it for herself. "You can't be serious! This isn't happening! Deon?!"

Deon stood up from his desk, cleared his throat and said, "Hello Tammy, nice to see you again."

Tammy looked at Mark and back to Deon, "Motherfucker, your fly is open!" Tears running down her face, Tammy felt like she was about to pass out. She couldn't believe what she was seeing.

Mark began to speak, "Baby, this isn't what it looks like." He tried to console his wife.

"Then please tell me what it is. What is it, huh? You open the door looking nervous, this motherfucker's pant is unzipped and this damn office smell like shit!" By this time, a small crowd had gathered in front of Deon's office. "Don't insult my intelligence Mark, tell me the truth! You were in here having sex with Deon!"

"No Tammy, that's not true, we were having a meeting." Mark looked at Deon to make sure that he would agree with his story.

Tammy walked towards her husband, rubbed his face. "Is that right baby? You were having a meeting? You weren't in here fucking a man? That's what you're telling me, right baby?" She hauled off and slapped him with everything that she had in her. "I asked you not to play with my intelligence. If you were having a meeting, where are the notes? Why isn't there a computer on? Do you really think that I'm that stupid

Mark?! You've been married to me for five years! Five! You should know I'm not that stupid!"

The small crowd outside of Deon's office was snickering. Tammy looked up and saw Mark's assistant smirking. "I really thought that it was you. All this time, I thought it was you, and for that, I apologize. But that smirk on your face lets me know that you knew all this time and you're happy that I found out." The assistant said nothing.

"Tammy." Deon began to speak, "I'm sorry, please, can we talk about this somewhere else? You're embarrassing yourself."

"I'm embarrassing myself?! I just caught you and my husband……wait……who was sucking whose dick?" Who's' the giver and who's the receiver?"

"Tammy please!" Mark said.

"Please what?! Oh, am I embarrassing you? Did you not want the entire office to know that you're having sex with a man?

Well, too bad! Now they know!" Tammy began to think about their children, and she began to cry a little harder. "Our children, what am I supposed to tell our children? I can't do this; I just can't do this." She walked out, got on the elevator and let out the loudest scream that she could.

Mark looked at the crowd and said, "The show is over, you all can go back to work now. My wife was just overreacting." He was still trying to clean up what was evident to everyone. He took a slow walk back to his office and called his assistant in. "Did that make you feel good?" He asked her.

"I have no idea what you're talking about."

"Don't play coy with me. I know you probably told Tammy exactly where she could find me." You see, in the beginning, Mark was indeed sleeping with his assistant and broke it off with her when he started seeing his colleague Deon. "You are bitter because I stopped dealing with you and today a perfect opportunity presented itself for your revenge."

His assistant, laughed, "Mark, trust me, it would have given me great pleasure to spill your little secret, but it wasn't me. Tammy stumbled upon you by mistake. Am I happy that it happened? Yes, I am. Now, is there anything else that I can help you with? I have work to do." She didn't even give him a chance to respond.

Mark sat at his desk for a while, trying to figure out what he was going to do. How was he going to get out of this and then he thought about what Tammy said, *what would he tell his children?* His precious little girls. He was sorry that Tammy found out like this, but he was happy that she had found out. They hadn't loved each other in a long time, and they both knew it. They stayed together for as long as they did for the kids' sake. He began to cry because he knew that this would surely hurt his daughters and they were the most important of all.

# **<u>Chapter 3</u>**

Tammy drove home in a rage, crying and yelling and mind racing a million miles a minute. She knew that Mark was cheating, but with a man! This is totally unacceptable. Why was this hurt so different from him cheating with a woman? She didn't know, but she knew that it hurt, a gut punch that knocked the wind out of her, that she was still trying to catch her breath from. It was almost time to pick the girls up from school, so she was trying to get herself together.

Later that night, Mark comes home, he didn't see Tammy right away, so he went straight upstairs to see the girls. "Daddy!" They both yelled. "We missed you." It was like they talked in unison all the time.

"Hey daddy's little princesses, I've missed you too." There was sadness in his voice and tears in his eyes. "What's wrong daddy? Why are you crying?" One of the little girls asked.

"Oh, I just missed you both so much, and these tears are tears of joy because I'm finally home." They both smiled, and the girls began to wipe their dad's face. "Well, I know that it's almost bedtime, so you guys better get ready before mom comes in. Little did he know that Tammy was standing behind him the entire time. Marked turned around and thought he saw a ghost. He kissed his little ladies good night and walked downstairs while Tammy got the girls settled for bed.

Tammy didn't reach the bottom step well before Mark began to speak. She held her hands up because she didn't want to hear it. She pointed towards a half bottle of wine that she had sitting on the counter, "I need more wine, before I hear anything that you have to say so that I can stay calm…and before you open your mouth, all I want to hear is the truth; I don't want to hear any bullshit. You owe me that much."

Mark cleared his throat, at this point truth was all that he had left. "First, I want to say that I'm sorry. I know that probably means nothing, but truly I'm sorry. I don't even know where to start with this."

"From the beginning would be good, try that; you're right, your *I'm sorry*, don't mean shit. Continue." She says as she raises her glass towards him.

Mark sighs and shakes his head. "It didn't start out with Deon. You were right from the beginning; I was sleeping with my assistant. That quickly became a mess and the buzz spread quickly over the office."

"So you decided to start another office romance, with a guy no less, would be a smart thing to do?" Tammy started laughing very loud. "You have got to be the dumbest nigga, I know." Tammy put her glass of wine down and picked up the bottle and began to drink from it. "Seriously, what made you think that was a good idea, huh?

"Tammy, please this is hard enough, please stop making it harder. Let me get this out, please. As I was saying, it did start with my assistant, but she was becoming obsessive like I was married to her. We always had to have lunch together, if she saw me talking to any other woman in the office, she got jealous and thought that I was trying to sleep with them, so I broke it off with her. I honestly don't know how this thing with Deon started. All I know is that it progressed quickly, and I was in another office romance."

"With a guy, a damn man!"

"Are you going to keep saying that? Yes, Tammy, a man, a man! Does it matter?!"

"Yes, it matters! You took away my right to choose! I didn't have a choice in the matter."

"You aren't making any sense. You knew that I was cheating on you with a woman, did I not take away your right to choose then?"

"I can't compete with a man!"

"So you have a problem with gay people?"

"Hell no and you know that Mark! My damn stylist is gay! But I'm not married to him; I'm married to your disrespectful ass. If that's the type of life that they choose to live, go for it! I would have respected you more if you came to me, sat me down and told me, but this shit is unacceptable! Your office! I caught you right in your office, Mark. It's like you didn't care if people knew, you had me looking stupid!"

"Cheating is cheating; it doesn't matter if it's with a man or a woman." Mark walked around in a circle for a while. "Tammy, what's done is done, and I'm sorry. How many times do you want me to say that I'm sorry?"

"So, are you gay, straight, bi-sexual, or what?"

"I'm not gay, just because I was with a man, doesn't make me gay or bi-sexual."

"Oh my God, do you know how stupid you sound right now? Mark, you were having sex with a guy, what does that make you?!

"I have never allowed another man to penetrate me, so I'm not gay!"

"So, you sucking his dick doesn't make you gay either? Make me understand Mark." Tammy sat down on a stool and propped her hand under her chin because this she had to hear.

"I'm not gay dammit! Stop saying that. Look, it obvious we aren't going to resolve this, so I'm going to bed, we can talk about this another time." Mark began to walk towards the stairs.

"The hell you say. You've been staying out, take your ass right back to where ever it is that you've been laying your head and I will make up another lie in the morning to tell the children."

"Please, I'm tired, it's been a long day, and it will be an even longer day tomorrow."

"What the fuck does that have to do with me? Just so that we are VERY clear, I will be filing for a divorce first thing in the morning, and I will have full custody of the kids."

"Like hell, you will. I love my kids, and you know that! Let's not forget that you are cheating too. If you want a divorce, fine, but you aren't taking my children away from me. This is still my home too, I will sleep downstairs on the couch, but I'm not going anywhere tonight."

The next couple of days Mark was at home every night like a faithful husband because he knew sooner rather than later, he would no longer be seeing his girls every night. Divorce is a bittersweet thing, but it happens. Truth be told, they should have gotten a divorce a long time ago, besides they both were cheating and the marriage was already dysfunctional. How many people can attest to the fact that they stay together in loveless marriages, cheating marriages, even abusive marriages all because of the children?

You are not helping your children by staying in these types of marriages. Ask yourself these questions, what am I teaching my children? That it's ok to stay with someone that cheats; repeatedly? It's ok to stay with someone that hits you? It's ok to stay with someone that you wake up to every morning that doesn't have two words to say to you for months? Believe it or not, your children are smarter than you give them credit for. They see the unhappiness, they hear the silent yelling, and they see the silent tears. If you've done all you can do, prayer and counseling included, when is it time to let go? What LIES are you hiding beneath that smile?

*The Rather's*

# **<u>Chapter 1</u>**

"Bitch find your way home," Taylor yelled to his wife as she got out of the car to go to work. Taylor was selfish and self-centered, his wife Lola questioned herself daily as to what in the world made her marry him. In the two years that they dated prior to marriage, they argued like cats and dogs, yet a marriage somehow happened. Taylor dropped Lola off at work every morning, driving her car that he didn't help pay for, yet he had the nerve to have an attitude when she requested that he be on time for once to pick her up.

"I tell you what, don't be here in time to pick me up. I will call the police and report my car stolen!" Taylor sped off in the two thousand Honda Accord. *Lord, why did I marry this man? I regret it every single day of my life. I am tired of being*

*embarrassed in front of my job every day. People have to wait*

*for me because my ride is not here or they have to hear this*

*yelling every morning.*

"Good morning girl," one of her co-workers said to her as Lola walked into the building.

Trying her very best to smile, Lola managed a very dry, "Good morning." She was so embarrassed because she knew that her co-worker saw and heard everything that just happened.

"Don't give me that dry good morning. Don't take it out on me because you have to deal with that idiot." Sam was one of the ones at her job that she actually liked and got along with and she didn't mind telling Lola exactly how she felt about Taylor.

"Girl, it's so embarrassing, I'm so sick of him I don't know what to do. Every day, he drops me off, in my car, ride around all day doing God knows what and has the nerve to get an attitude when I ask him to be on time to pick me up from work."

"Lola, you are so much better than this. I see you come in here every day, stressed, fighting through tears: yeah, I hear you in the bathroom sometimes doing a silent cry. What makes you stay with someone who doesn't treat you right?"

"What else is out there Sam? I see you too, dating guy after guy, giving your all, for it not to work out in the end." Sam gave her the side-eye. "You dated Tommy for five years! Five and it all went to hell! You thought he was the one until you found out about his other family across town. I still can't believe that one."

"Neither can I! But at least, I put myself back out there; I'm not afraid to start over and give love another try. I deal with the situation, and I move on. I can't tell you what to do, but this; what I see before me daily, has to stop."

Sam and Lola put their conversation on hold and went to work. After a day of dealing with rude, angry customers, all Lola wanted to do was go home, put her feet up and relax. "It's five o clock, hurry up and lock the doors," Sam said.

"Well, dang lil mommy, you have somewhere to be?"

"Aren't you nosey, but yes! I have a date with this guy named Jason that I met. He's too cute for words."

"Yet another one huh? Don't reply to that, let's get finished so that I can go home. I'm tired, and I'm sure you will tell me all about it tomorrow." After closing out all the reports for the day and locking up, Lola walked out to Taylor not being there yet again.

"You want me to give you a ride home, girl?"

"No Sam, that's ok, go home and get ready for your hot date."

"You know that I can't leave you out here by yourself, so get your butt in the car. Besides, if you stand out here, I have to stand with you, which will make me late, so let's go."

Lola looked around once again to see if Taylor is maybe turning the corner before getting in Sam's car. "Thanks, girl, I really appreciate it. Have fun on your date."

As Lola was stepping out of the car, who comes rolling up but Taylor.

"You had me rushing to come get you on time, and you weren't even there! I had to stop what I was doing just to get you, and you found a ride home. Why can't she bring you home every day?"

Lola took a deep breath, shut Sam's door, waved goodbye and walked in the house. Taylor followed her, still yelling. "First of all, it's not her responsibility to give me a ride home every day! Secondly, you are driving MY CAR! Thirdly, what in the hell do you have to do that's so important all day that you can't pick me up on time? Last but not least, I will drive myself to work so that we don't have this problem! I'm sick of arguing with you about the same thing day in and day out with your disrespectful ass! Acting a fool in front of my job and shit! I'm sick of you Taylor! I want a divorce!"

"A divorce over me not picking you up on time? You can't be serious. Fine, I will have them put a rush on getting my car repaired." Taylor's car was in the shop for about four months, because he was getting the inside of it chromed out, custom leather seats, the works. If you haven't guessed it by now, Taylor was a well-known drug dealer, but he never worked a corner a day in his life. It was all glitz and glamour when Lola and Taylor first started dating. The typical good girl, bad boy syndrome. At first, she didn't know what he was into because he didn't get calls all times of the night, he never hung out late nights, but he did take a lot of trips and sometimes she went with him. She just thought that he was just a "rich kid" and spoiling her with a lot of weekend getaways until she discovered a suitcase in his closet one day filled with cocaine. She questioned him about it, and Taylor told her that he was holding it for a friend and it was just a one-time thing. Naive, she believed him, but she was scared to death until he got it out of the house. That just made Taylor move differently, but the money and trips kept coming so Lola knew that he was still in the business.

"You really think that this is about you not picking me up on time? Really Taylor?"

"Then what else is it?"

Lola stood there with her face in her hands, shaking her head. She was about to tell him everything that she knew. "I blame myself; I blame myself for sticking by your disrespectful, cheating, raggedy ass?!"

"I have never cheated on you Lola! Never!"

Lola went to the guest bedroom, pulled out a folder and laid all the pictures, emails and cell phone calls that she had out for him to see. "I know about the baby." She went into the kitchen and poured herself a glass of wine. Taylor was standing there in disbelief.

"So you had me followed! You sneaky, undercover bitch!"

"There's that word again. There you go trying to play the victim again. No Taylor, I didn't have you followed, I don't have the time nor the energy for that. You see, for as much as an asshole you are, I trusted you. No, no, no, Tonya; you know Tonya right? She decided to pay me a visit at my job one day. Apparently, she got tired of waiting for you to tell me that you were leaving me, to be with her and the baby. When were you going to tell me? Huh?"

"Baby, I can explain." Still fumbling through the evidence that Lola had laid before him.

"Baby? What happened to the bitch? She's beautiful by the way. She even brought the baby by to see me. That day, I cried off and on in the bathroom all day. Not sure if I wanted to come home and kill you or just pack all my shit and leave." Lola's voice grew very calm. "Stupid me, thinking that maybe, just maybe you would come clean and tell me everything."

"It's out now Lola! It's out! What you wanna do, because I don't have time for this dramatic scene that you're giving me." Lola stood up, drank what was left of her wine and threw the glass at Taylor. "Bitch, are you crazy?!"

"There he is, there is the Taylor that I know! Yes, I'm crazy; crazy for loving your sorry ass all these years! Sticking by a raggedy motherfucker who has no respect for me!" Lola started throwing everything that she could get her hands on.

"Man, Lola stop!" Getting out of the way of every object that was being thrown at him. "What do you want me to do? Hunh? She's here now, what do you want me to do?"

"Get your disrespectful, rude ass out! Getcho shit and go to your baby momma! Let her put up with your nasty ass! Without hesitation, Taylor left.

# __Chapter 2__

Two weeks had passed, and Lola had not seen or heard from Taylor. As much as she hated him at the moment, she still wondered if he was alright. "I'm looking for a Lola Rather." A young man holding some flowers said.

"I will take them." Sam jumped up to retrieve them.

"Sign here, please. Have a nice day."

"These are beautiful," Sam says as she was smelling the flowers and walking them over to Lola's desk. "Here girl, these were sent to you."

Lola quickly started looking for a card to see who they were from. "Ah ha, there it is." She opened the card and was surprised as to who they were from. The card read: *Lola, thank you for raising a man. Sincerely, Tonya.* Lola was furious!

"Well, hell girl who are they from? You look pissed"! Lola couldn't speak. Sam grabbed the card from her hand and started reading it. "Who the hell is Tonya?!" Lola didn't tell anyone about Taylor's child.

"That would be Taylor's child's mother." She managed to get it out through gritted teeth.

"I know I didn't just hear what I think I heard. It's who?!"

"Not now Sam, this is not the time or place."

"Well, tonight is the time, and it's happening nowhere else than the bar."

They continued about their work day, but Lola could not get it out of her head that Tonya actually had the nerve to send her flowers. As hard as she tried to get the thoughts out of her mind, she couldn't, so she picked up her phone and sent Taylor a text. *Listen, I'm not bothering ya'll over there, so please tell your baby mommy to stop being petty.* Taylor sent a question mark back. Lola took a picture of the card and flowers and sent it to him. No reply.

"Girl, it's been a long day, I can't wait to hit somebody's bar! I need a drink or three."

"Beat you to the parking lot," Sam says to her friend. She got to the parking lot and stopped in the tracks. "Hell no!"

Looking back at Lola. "And you better not think about talking to his sorry ass!"

Lola looked up and spotted Taylor. She tried ignoring him and walked straight to her car, but that didn't work. "Lola, Lola. Slow down, let me talk to you for a minute."

"We don't have anything to talk about Taylor." Reaching for her door.

"At least let me apologize."

"Are you serious right now? Don't come to my job with this."

"Lola please, I love you, and I am genuinely sorry for everything that I've done." Lola didn't say anything, and she didn't know what to say or if she could believe anything that he was saying. "Baby please, can we go somewhere and talk about this? Please?"

"Taylor, how many times have I heard this from you? What happened, you got tired of playing in-house with Tonya or did she get tired of your bullshit and put you out?" Lola was waiting for Taylor to spew a few foul words from his mouth because she wasn't making it easy for him; she wasn't letting him have his way.

"I've had a lot of time to think since I've been out of the house; and I haven't been spending all my nights at Tonya's."

"Is that supposed to make me feel better?  Who else is there?  You know what, never mind, it's none of my business." Almost snatching the door off the hinges of her car, Lola was furious! Taylor didn't try to stop her; it was at that moment that he realized that it was going to take a lot more than *I'm sorry, baby I won't do it anymore*, to get through to Lola this time. For the next few weeks, there were numerous flower, balloon bouquet and candy deliveries to Lola's house as well as her job.

"Well, well, well, isn't he going all out trying to win you over?" Sam questioned.

"Yes, he really is.  I think that he's serious this time, he seems to be really sorry.  I haven't seen this side of Taylor in a very long time."

"Look, Lola, I can't tell you what to do, what I will say is, if you are considering taking him back, make sure that he is

FOR REAL and not just being sweet to get you back. I've seen it done before."

"I appreciate that you are that friend that does not mind giving it to me straight, no matter how much I hate it sometimes."

"Straight, no chaser. I love you Lola, and I just want what's best for you, but you're a grown woman, and you are going to do what you want to regardless of what I say....but I wouldn't be a true friend if I didn't say it."

"I know, and I love you for it. Trust me, I'm not taking this lightly. Taylor did a lot of damage to our relationship and a few weeks of flowers can't make up for years of disrespect and a WHOLE BABY, but he's trying. We will see what happens."

# **Chapter 3**

Lola went home that night to find Taylor laying on her doorstep, beaten and bloody! She dropped everything in her hands and ran over to him, "Oh my God, what happened?! Who did this to you?!" Screaming for help, trying to get Taylor to talk and fumbling for her phone to call 911. "Taylor, talk to me, please. Baby, wake up, Taylor!"

The 911 operator came on the line, "You're through to 911, how can I help you?"

"Help me please!"

"Ma'am, are you hurt? Where are you?"

Lola was crying uncontrollably that she could barely get the words out.  She and Taylor were not on the best of terms, but she still loved him. "No, it's, it's my husband. He's in front of our house."  She looked at Taylor and began to cry a little harder; still shaking him trying to get him to wake up.

"Ma'am, where are you?"

"Please help me, he won't wake up, he won't wake up. Please."

"Ma'am, tell me where you are so that I can send someone to help your husband."

"2779 Chestnut Ave, please send someone, please hurry."

"Help is on the way, ma'am. Try to stay calm; help is on the way."

Taylor coughed, "He's awake, he's awake!  Taylor, Taylor what happened?"  He was too weak to say anything.

"Help is on the way, just hang in there." Lola was trying to get herself together, but it was very hard. She sat next to him and held his hand until the paramedics arrived. They rushed Taylor to the nearest hospital and immediately began to work on him. Lola had what seemed like a million people around her, asking what happened. She didn't have answers for the police, doctors or nurses because she didn't know herself. All she knew was she found him passed out, bloody, beaten and she was scared to death.

After hours of waiting, a doctor came out to give Lola an update. He let out a loud sigh before he began talking. "Hi, I'm Dr. Bennett." He extended his hand to Lola. "I'm going to be honest with you, things look pretty bad. Whoever did this to him, did not intend for him to live." Lola started sobbing, Dr. Bennett rubbed her arm. "He has several broken ribs, his jaw is broken, and he has so much internal bleeding. We will monitor him very closely for the next couple of hours and see what happens. I assure you that we are doing everything that we can to ensure that he gets through this. Is there anyone that you can call?"

Through her tears, she said, "No, he's an only child, and his parents died when he was young."

"Is there someone that you can call to be here with you?"

"Um, yes, my friend Samantha. Dr. Bennett, when I can I see him? I just want to see him."

"Give us a few minutes to get him situated in a room and I will have someone come out and get you. Hang in there."

He rubbed her arm again to give her some comfort. Lola couldn't talk, she just shook her head. While Lola waited for someone to come out and get her, she called Sam and briefly explained what happened, without hesitation, Sam was there.

"Oh hunnie, are you ok? Of course, you aren't ok." Sam says as she hugs her friend. "What in the world is going on?"

"I don't know, I came home and found him on our doorstep." One of the nurses came out to let Lola know that she could go in to see Taylor. "Will you come with me?"

"Oh, of course, I will." They walked into the room, and they both gasped! There were cords, wires and machines everywhere. His face had swollen to the point where they couldn't recognize him. "My word, who could do such a thing?" Lola was shivering and crying. "It's going to be ok Lola; it's going to be ok. You have to be strong for him, pray and have faith that he's going to make it through this thing." Lola gathered herself because she knew that Sam was right. It was going to be hard, but she was going to see Taylor through this.

# Chapter 4

Taylor spent a month in the hospital, with Lola by his side every step of the way. They released him, and she took him home with her. After getting him settled and allowing him to rest for a few days, Lola began to question Taylor as to what happened and how he got to their house. "Taylor, do you remember what happened? How did you get here? I've had the police questioning me for the last month, and I am just as clueless as they are."

"I don't really remember a lot of it. I remember leaving Tonya's house because I was dropping the baby off, I stopped to help a woman that had a flat tire and the next thing I know, I was being punched from every direction."

"Wow, and you've never seen this woman before? Do you remember what she looks like?"

"Can we talk about this tomorrow, I'm really tired, and I just want to rest."

She smiled, "Sure, get some rest, we'll talk more tomorrow."

Taylor grabbed Lola's hand, "Thank you. I really mean that; I don't know where I would be if it weren't for you."

"Sure, no problem." Lola was a little thrown off by Taylor's story, something just wasn't adding up, but she let it go. For the next few weeks, Lola had police officers in and out of their home because they were trying to figure out what happened to Taylor. They were coming up empty, Taylor told them the same story that he told Lola. After a while, they stopped coming around, and things were becoming back to normal. Taylor was moving around like his old self, but with a better attitude. He and Lola seemed as if they were going to work things out and live the life that she always wanted.

One Saturday morning while they were having breakfast, there was a knock at the door. "I'll get it," Taylor said. He opened the door and to his surprise it was Tonya. "Tonya, what are you doing here?" Lola flew out of her chair and to the front door.

"Nice to see you too," Tonya replied, with much attitude. "I'm here because of her; you do remember her right, your daughter."

And before Taylor could answer, Lola had a few questions of her own. "Where have you been for the past few months? I've called you and left several messages with no reply."

"I don't owe you or him an explanation; I'm here for my daughter." Lola looked at the little girl that Tonya was holding. She looked and smelled like she hadn't taken a bath in days. Come to think of it; Tonya looked the same way.

"What about her," Taylor asked? "You could have at least brought my daughter to see me if you knew that I wasn't able to come see her. What do you want Tonya?"

"She needs clothes; it's getting cold."

"Now that I'm up and moving around, I will make sure that she has everything that she needs, just give me a few days."

"Why can't you just give me the money? I can go to the store now and get what she needs."

Taylor began to look a little closer at Tonya, "Are you high?!"

"Don't insult me!"

"It's not an insult because I was wondering the same thing," Lola chimed in.

"Bitch, why are you even talking?"

"You showed up at my door, rang my doorbell with your rude ass and you have the nerve to ask me why I'm talking?"

"Stop it!" Taylor yelled. "Look, Tonya, I said give me a couple of days, and I will make sure that she has everything that she needs.

"Well, what am I supposed to do until then?"

"What have you been doing this past couple of months?"

"Getting by, but now I don't have to because her dad is better. If you don't have the money, get it from her." Nodding her head towards Lola.

"You must be high if you think I'm about to give you some money, bitch I didn't get you pregnant."

Before Tonya had a chance to say anything, Taylor repeated himself once more, "I said give me a few days. That's it; I'm not going to say it anymore." He didn't give Tonya or Lola the chance to say anything else before shutting the door.

"I agree that you shouldn't have given her any money, but you didn't have to shut the door in her face. She was holding your daughter after all."

"Drop it, Lola."

"No. I will not drop it. Your child's mother shows up here of all places, asking for money, looking and smelling like she doesn't know what soap and water is and you tell me to drop it. The part that's really bothering me is the fact that not one time did you interact with your daughter."

"Yes, Lola, drop it." Taylor's old attitude was peeking out.

"What's really going on Taylor?"

"Damn it, Lola, just drop it!"

"No! I want answers, and I want them now!"

"Why you gotta always do this? Things were going good and you have to go fuck them up."

Lola could not believe what she was hearing, "Are you kidding me? I messed things up?! Well, welcome back Taylor."

"You want the truth? Here it is, the day that I dropped the baby back off at Tonya's, there was another guy there. I asked who he was for the safety of my daughter and things went way left. He informed me that he was, in fact, the father of the baby and that he could prove it. I was questioning Tonya when the dude hit me across my head."

"For what?!"

"Tonya was dating him before I started messing with her. When I came around, the dude had just gotten locked up. She was playing both of us. She was still in a relationship with him, writing him, taking the baby to visit him, all of that. Anyway, I managed to get out of the house and made it here, I was going to tell you everything, but he followed me. That's how I ended up at your front door. I don't know what Tonya told him, but I remember him saying something about me pimping her out and having her strung out."

"So she is on drugs? If you know who did it, why didn't you just tell the police?

"I guess, I don't know. I've never seen her taking it, and I've never given her anything. You didn't believe me when I told you that I wasn't spending that many nights over there. Tonya started acting differently when I was there, that's why I was surprised when you sent me the picture of the flowers and card that you got from her. She was trying to get a reaction out of you because I was barely there. I don't need the police involved because no matter what you think, I do care about the baby and you. I know she's not mine, but I have a bond with her, and it's going to be a little hard to break. The way that guy beat me within an inch of my life, I don't want him coming back here to try and do anything to you if I tell the police what happened and that's the truth, about everything."

Lola sat there for a few minutes in disbelief at what she just heard. "Taylor, for months, my life could have been in danger, while you were lying in bed, not being able to defend yourself or me, you should have told me so that I could have been prepared."

"I don't think that he was going to do anything. Besides, I'm having it taken care of."

"What does that mean?"

"Nothing, the less you know, the better off you will be."

"If you cry more than you smile, it's time to let go." ~ **Coco**

www.ingramcontent.com/pod-product-compliance
Lightning Source LLC
Chambersburg PA
CBHW030634130626
46552CB00002B/838